My Dentist, My Friend

Written and illustrated by

P.K. Hallinan

*For Lin Mattson,
whose friendship has never
needed a filling.*

Ideals Children's Books • Nashville, Tennessee

Published by Ideals Children's Books
An imprint of Hambleton-Hill Publishing, Inc.
Nashville, Tennessee 37218

Printed and bound in the United States of America

Library of Congress Cataloging-in-Publication Data

Hallinan, P.K.
    My dentist, my friend / written and illustrated by P.K. Hallinan.
      p.   cm.
    Summary: A visit to the dentist is shown to be nothing to fear.
    ISBN 1-57102-086-1 (paper)
    [1. Dentists—Fiction. 2. Dental care—Fiction. 3. Teeth—Care
and hygiene—Fiction. 4. Stories in rhyme.] I. Title.
PZ8.3.H15My   1996
[E]—dc20   95-37592
                                                           CIP
                                                            AC

My dentist, my friend—
what more can I say?
My dentist has helped me
to smile this way!

Yes, dentists are helpful
in all that they do.
They keep our teeth clean—
and healthier too!

When we go to the dentist,
we usually will find
a lobby that's hopping
with sights of all kinds.

There are children with toys.
There are parents with books.
There are dental assistants
with welcoming looks.

And music plays lazily
filling the halls
as everyone waits
for their name to be called.

The next thing we know. . .
we're ready to go!

The oral hygienist shows kindness and care as we're led to a room with a big, comfy chair.

We hop right on up,
with a bib 'round our neck,
and a very bright light
inspects every speck.

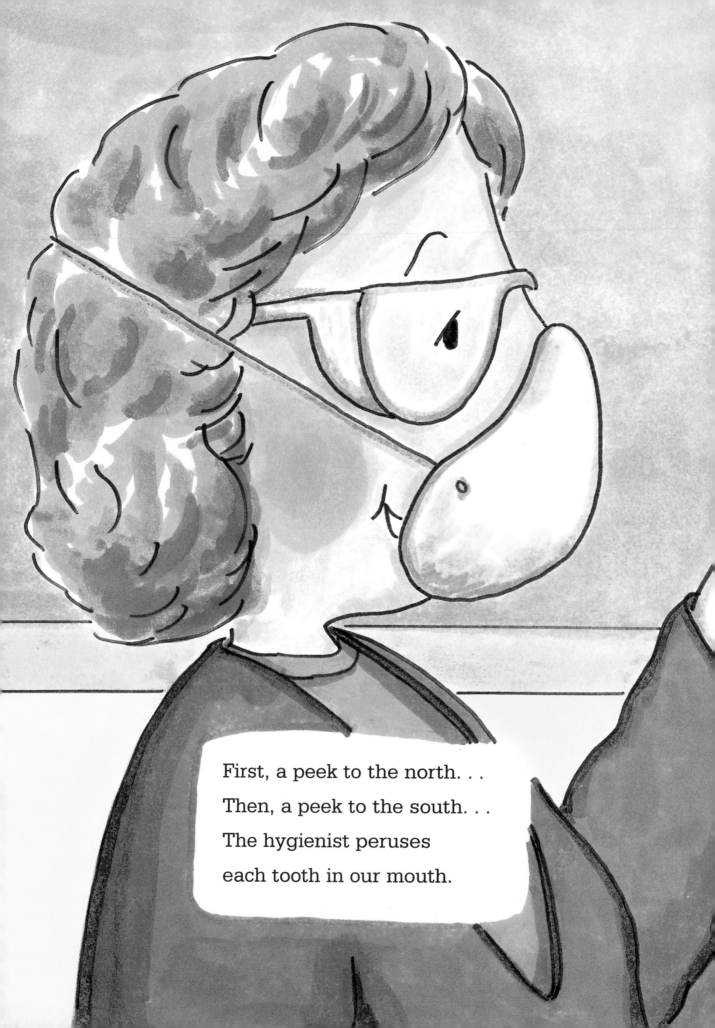

First, a peek to the north. . .
Then, a peek to the south. . .
The hygienist peruses
each tooth in our mouth.

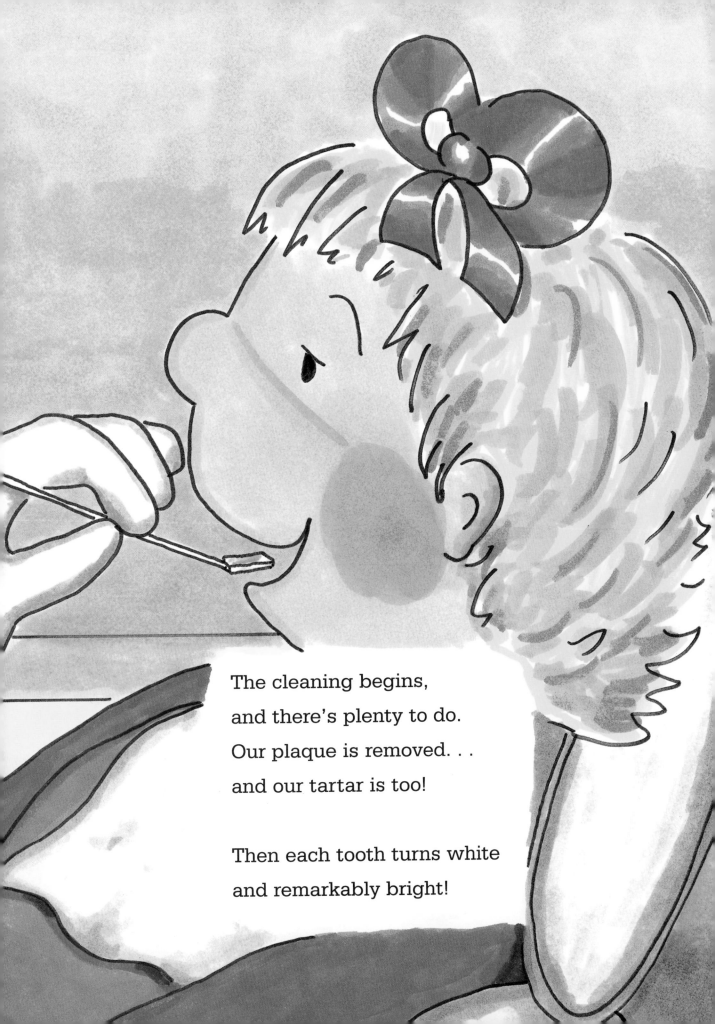

The cleaning begins,
and there's plenty to do.
Our plaque is removed. . .
and our tartar is too!

Then each tooth turns white
and remarkably bright!

At last comes the dentist,
when the cleaning is through,
for a gentle exam
and a thoughtful review.

The dentist is thorough
and takes a long look—
inspecting for cavities
and checking each nook.

We might need some x-rays,
but that's kind of fun.
We wear a lead apron,
and suddenly—we're done!

We're given a toothbrush,
some floss, and some praise,
'cause regular brushing
kept cavities away.

And they send us along
with a ten-gallon smile
that's good for six months—
well, at least for a while.

Yes, dentists *are* helpful—
there's really no doubt.
Their care and concern
are what friendship's about.

So, I guess there's no question
why I trust and depend
on this *special* person. . .